The Center Ring

!!! * INVITATION *** !!!**

* * * * * * * * *

You are cordially invited to a **celebration**—

a celebration in the ***Great Cosmic Dance!***

Time: Now — and from here on out!

Place: Here — and wherever. . .

Be sure to bring: dreams, stardust, magic wands, crystal balls — any and all such items. . .

Enter: the world of the Clown, The Fool, the Jester!

Love, **Argus**

Love, **Blue**

The Center Ring

Pat Barner

and

Judy Vermillion-Witt

Standard Disclaimer (sort of)

The names we are using in our book have been changed to protect the innocent (or the guilty). That caption is provided in most books we have read. Remember, this is a clown book. Have the names really been changed? How many times will you see yourself?

Photography processing and procedures by Joel Becker. Original creative designs for photography by Judy Vermillion-Witt.

Hampton Roads Publishing Company, Inc.
891 Norfolk Square
Norfolk, VA 23502
Or call: (804)459-2453
(FAX: (804)455-8907

If you are unable to order this book from your local bookseller, you may order directly from the publisher. Call 1-800-766-8009, toll-free.

ISBN 1-878901-31-1

10 9 8 7 6 5 4 3 2 1

Printed in the United States of America

Appreciation And Acknowledgements

Special thanks to Harriet Schley, our editor, who took the time to wade through manuscripts, notes, and tapes to edit, correct, and make sense of the writings of four people; Pat and Judy, Argus and Blue.

Joel Becker, one terrific clown photographer, who gave of his visual wizardry to create the magical visions of this book.

Jack Witt, who believed in us enough to make our dream come true.

Dedication

Argus and Blue dedicate this book to all the grown-ups who still believe there is magic and wonder in the world.

My portion of our book is dedicated to my family for believing amidst the gales of laughter from the upstairs studio that we really were working on our book; for surviving being picked up at school by a van full of clowns; for unselfish support and pride in my work. With all my love to my family and friends,

Pat

To my father who invented, imagined, and created the "Scrabbit Rabbit" stories for our nightly bedtime adventures together, and who I am sure, is woven into the very nature of my friend, Argus.

And to Mrs. Lavender, my third-grade teacher who opened me to the world of art. It was in her third-grade class I made papier-mache pots for Thanksgiving, drew pastel murals of seasonal changes, and won first prize for a collage of Snow White and Seven Dwarfs. To their creativity and imagination which ignited my own, I dedicate this work,

Judy

Table of Contents

"People say that what we're all seeking is a meaning for life. I don't think that's what we're really seeking. I think that what we're seeking is an experience of being alive, so that our life experiences on the purely physical plane will have resonances within our own innermost being and reality, so that we actually feel the rapture of being alive."

Joseph Campbell
The Power of Myth

Introduction

Explaining the Unexplainable

We are writing this book to share our adventures, discoveries and experiences in being clowns and to tell how we have used clowning as a tool for self-growth and self- discovery for ourselves and others.

It is not *the* way, but *a* way for opening the locked up heart to our inner Child—that part of us long neglected in the process of "growing up."

We use this tool to—balance between opposites within ourselves,
express our most creative selves,
and communicate with others.

As clowns we learn how to see,
how to feel,
and how to speak on
a deeper level.

Through silence and mime, we develop the skills of listening and responding in a simple and direct manner.

We discover laughter to be a great healer—that ability to laugh at ourselves in a world filled with absurdities. Laughter helps us to forget ourselves so that we may find ourselves.

Clowning helps us remember what it feels like
to lie in damp green grasses and gaze into a midnight star-studded sky,
or how it was to watch butterflies dance on hollyhocks,
or feel the warmth of a summer morning as we "toe dipped" at ocean's edge.

As adults we have forgotten to wonder, to stand in awe of the creation around us. We have neglected our participation as creative, beautiful beings, born into a grand universal theme.

The clown invites us to experience the world with trust and encourages us to expand our horizons. We use this symbol of the clown to enhance our personal growth, and offer it as a tool for self-growth and exploration to be used by counselors, patients, clergy, and those truly remarkable people who want to take advantage of all life has to offer.

We have used our clown workshop for groups of people in therapy, for instance. Often support groups of Adult Children of Alcoholics take our day-long workshop on Beginning Clowning because they realize they never had much of a chance to be children. They take this workshop together to mend old wounds and to continue to support one another.

One such class was special because the therapist participated as well. Recognizing the fearful anticipation of her clients, and feeling a bit uneasy herself, she took the risk of including herself in the day. She played, put on costume and makeup with her patients, and for that day was not therapist but fellow child, sharing the same experiences. During the end of the day processing her clients shared how meaningful the whole day was for them, but especially so because their counselor participated with them. In turn she was also able to share how frightened she initially was, to be with them without her mask of "being professional." The trust that formed from that experience enhanced the group's therapy and helped them be a more supportive system for one another.

As Pat and Judy, we have learned through the eyes of Blue and Argus to see an invisible bond grow into a deep and loving relationship. From that bond we tell our story.

Choosing

Colors

To fingerpaint

Shows the

Values

of

our

life.

Blue.

I.

Creativity

ENTER INTO THE CENTER RING: Pat and Judy. Two ordinary women—each struggling with the frustrations of everyday living: jobs, children, households, spouses. Each struggling with the burning creativity within—creativity demanding to be recognized and acknowledged as the inner core of our spirits. Yet we made choices, as so many do—to defer our desires to husbands' careers and children's interests.

ENTER INTO THE CENTER RING: two ordinary women

who experienced . . .TRANSFORMATION.

Deep within ourselves our talents to create and to affect people's lives started to spring forth. We began to live out what we created, and our journey began.

How many of us have suppressed our innate creative instincts without even realizing we were doing so? Parents, teachers, society in general have told us, and we have accepted:

"You can't do."—"You aren't good enough."

Many people have bought into this script, and, sadly, have never explored what else they might have been. Yet we, "ordinary women," found within ourselves the resources to tap into that creative source, and to live creatively in the world. We found our way into that world with great assistance from

!!!

Blue and Argus.

Family Portrait

"Time spent laughing is time spent with the gods."
—Japanese philosopher

Blue was not born without great labor pains. The labor of letting go of my rational, questioning, ever-doubting self was indeed painful. As far back as I can remember I told myself quite convincingly that I had no creative talents. I was told in the second grade, "You can't draw," and I had bought into that tape ever since. I never picked up a pencil to draw, or a crayon to color, unless I was helping my children. From this history, it was with difficulty but with faith that I asked for a dream—a dream that would reveal to me my own creative personality, my own distinct clown. It still amazes me how quickly it all came together when I was ready for the experience.

The clown as she appeared to me was dressed in pink. She was so totally feminine, yet so prissy-acting, it made me laugh. I saw the pink "farmer-john style" pants and shirt, the pink shoes. I watched as she fussed over her pink curls and ribbons and adjusted pink lace gloves. With amusement I realized she was certainly the other side of me: Pat Barner, who brushes her straight hair out of her face in the morning and rarely remembers to check it again. This clown stops at every reflective object to fix her hair and makeup!

I accepted this as truly mine and asked for a name. Of course it was obvious: "BLUE." Two important lessons I have been striving to learn, and which I find myself continuing to teach:

1. Things are not always as they seem.
2. Labels can be misleading.

When I am not clowning, I am working with people who have AIDS. Strange combination? Not really, for the clown gives me the courage to help other people live with their dying. Blue allows me to balance on the edge, which is what we try to do for anyone living with a life-threatening illness. We live on the edge, balancing hope for continued useful existence with acceptance that eventually we will all die.

Humor has been a valuable tool in working with people who are dying. In the thirteen years that I have been working with the dying, I have frequently used humor to break the constant stress and burden of sorrow. Sometimes all we can do is laugh at our own weaknesses, and it's a pleasant change from constant crying!

Blue's image often appears to me when I am at a crossroads trying to make a decision. Sometimes in our everyday living we feel helpless and not in control. At such times I ask Blue, "What would you do?" Answers and images always appear. When we tap into our most creative selves, even during difficulties, we make the right choices. For when we follow our intuitions with trust and with an open heart, we know we are where we are supposed to be.

Perhaps I was a clown long before I even realized it. Entertaining classmates in school with jokes and antics assured me a sense of peer acceptance.

Later, I nurtured my sense of humor, sometimes as my only resource in dealing with impossible situations. I remember one of my dying friends, Mona.

Mona and I had been casual friends throughout four years of our children's activities in school and in sports. The friendship became understandably closer as her body started to succumb to metastatic breast cancer.

I visited her weekly at the hospital. On her nightstand were several boxes from an expensive department store, beautiful nightgowns, gifts from the Officer's Wives' Club and other friends. The gowns remained in boxes and she always wore the old hospital gowns. After a couple of weeks I inquired about them, not realizing the fury I was unleashing by a "simple" question, "Why don't you wear those pretty gowns instead of the hospital ones?"

As I frequently remind people, those closest to the dying are the easiest targets for pent-up emotions. Mona gave it to me full force: "How dare you come in here every week looking so nice? How dare you tell me how to look?" Then a host of complaints and anger. I submitted meekly, stifling a desire to remind her I always visited on Sundays, which is the only day of the week I look nice!

Instead, I told her that I thought enough of her to dress up to see her, and she should think enough of me to do the same, pulling a childish pout, "You wouldn't like it if I came any old way." So we made a bargain, Mona and I, that next week we would look nice for each other.

Now, I knew my friend well enough to know how profound her depression was, and I knew she wouldn't make an effort to put on a nice gown. That week I showed up at the Naval hospital in my oldest robe, and large PINK(!!) fluffy slippers, with rollers in my hair and cold cream on my face.

This particular section of the hospital is a long ward of beds, Mona's being towards the end. Long before she saw me, she heard the ripple of laughter, for I made sure everyone saw me as I waved and informed them, "Hi! I'm Mona's friend. Hi! I'm here to see Mona. I'm Mona's friend." By the time I reached her bed, I was pretty proud of myself. Her face was scarlet as she demanded, "How could you do this to me?" I feigned innocence as I reminded her of our bargain. She hadn't kept her part, so I didn't dress up either. I did not stay very long that day, as neither of us was in the mood for any serious conversation.

I believed in the healing power of laughter even then. The next week, Mona was wearing one of her gowns. She had a bandanna on her head and was wearing makeup. I can tell you, she never looked more beautiful!

Argus:

I started by dreaming about clowns and studying about them. I discovered that artists had gone through phases of painting clowns. So why not be one?

I began by designing my own personal clown through "active imagination," whereby one sets a scene within the mind and writes about the imagery that appears.

> I am sitting in the forest beneath tall pine trees and gently swaying maple leaves. The earth smells soft and sweet. I touch the moss at my finger tips as I quietly anticipate the appearance of my imaginary playmate. I close my eyes. I linger and stretch out on green grasses and pine needles. A breeze blows over my face and I hear a drumming sound in the distance that grows louder and louder and moves behind the tree before me. "Hello," I call out. No answer. "Hello." The drumming sound changes into a kazoo tune. I begin to plead, "Please come out and talk to me. It's lonesome sitting here all alone." Still no answer. Suddenly, I see smoke rings rising beside the tree and disappearing into the treetops. "Look, we can't be friends if I can't see you." I put my head in my arms on the ground. I hear a rustling, shuffling sound in the grass. I lift my head and before my eyes, I see the *most* gorgeous gold tennis shoes I'd ever seen, and just above the shoes were white ruffles on large black tuxedo pants held up by wide suspenders. A large round pin was attached to them. The word "Argus" was written there. I sat upright and stared at his tuxedo shirt—each tuck covered in a different-colored ribbon, forming a rainbow across his chest. At his neck he wore a bright red bow tie, and a black top hat, decorated with Spring flowers, sat on his head. His white face had two red circles on his cheeks, a red-painted mouth, and a small red dot on the tip of his nose. His eyes twinkled beneath blue-painted eyebrows and his mouth turned upward into a smile. "My friend," I said. He nodded and bowed and handed me a red balloon. "LOVE" was written

> on it. The clown motioned for me to breathe into it, making it large and round. As I began to blow up the balloon, I glanced up to see my new friend skipping into the forest. He turned, blew me a kiss, waved and disappeared into the trees, playing the theme song of "Bridge Over the River Kwai" on his kazoo. "Come back soon so we can talk," I said. I returned the wave and the kiss as he skipped away.

Many conversations transpired throughout the years with Argus. I often sit with pen and paper speaking to him concerning difficult situations, seeking his advice. He soon became my Guide, who spoke to me of wiser thoughts and ways.

I later discovered that Argus was a mythological figure who had a hundred eyes that could see in a hundred directions at once. He was appointed by Zeus to guard his lover, whom he had changed into a cow.

Today, Argus is the brand name of a camera. When I clowned I carried a wooden toy camera with me to pretend to take people's pictures. As a professional artist, I began to carry my camera with me to photograph my surroundings. I had not done this before I met Argus. I realized recently that my art work was affected by new imagery. I was seeing in a new way and creating from a different source. Visually, I have become more aware of shadows, color, and light, and the connection between my eye and the eye of the camera. I began to see the beauty and wonder of the world around me, which enhances the creative expression of my life through art. My inner eye was being trained and sharpened by Argus the Clown and Argus the Camera!

Being Argus and Blue has taught us many lessons about who we are as people. Most important, we have become more open to change, the basis for creative living. As clowns, we are not professionals with titles, bound by expectations/limitations of our society. Rather, we image and create new resolutions and different approaches in a world of insecurities where nothing is absolute. In living as clowns, we have experienced life as an ongoing, ever-changing process.

TO LIVE CREATIVELY IS TO LIVE WITH CHANGE

Describe the House of your Imagination:

II.

Imagination

Imagine for a moment how your mind looks during its peak of creativity. See your brain as a honeycomb, with blue sky floating through the cells. Thought penetrates like a laser beam. These beams change the cells of the mind, refueling not only mind but body, not only body but soul.

See this honeycomb as a huge power plant supplying you with ideas, change and transference. When you are that close to your creative sense, you are that close to the Divine Spirit.

In our work we frequently meet therapists who describe imagination as the formation of a mental image which is neither real nor present. We watch them struggle to utilize their "left brains," the logical part of their minds, to the max. We gently urge them to allow the right side of the brain, the intuitive side, equal time. That way they will be able to use the gift of imagination in their work.

We find imagination is the ability to deal creatively with reality.

In the book *Lazaris, The Sacred Journey*, the author continually urges us to get "new pictures." Whether it be spirituality or love or work, our concepts are always changing. Frequently we hold on to old ideas and old memories, afraid to replace them, afraid we will have nothing to put in their place. But our world is constantly changing! Nothing is written in stone! Lazaris encourages us to get new pictures, to replace that which no longer serves us in a healthy manner with new pictures. The clown provides an avenue for creating new pictures, altering our views of the past, present and future.

Heeeeeeeere's Judy!!

Argus has helped me to imagine a more creative and fun-filled life. I grew up in a world where I was told that there was no future in being an artist, professionally or financially. Through the years, I believed what I was told, although an artist was what I most wanted to be. I began to paint more and more, even though it was only a hobby, until gradually I became aware that painting, mixing paints, and working in my studio were what made me happy, and gave me a sense of well-being. The thought of making money doing something I loved seemed absurd. I hesitated, I stuck to old beliefs and old patterns because they were safe and familiar.

Meanwhile, I developed Argus. Through being Argus, I also developed as a person. I practiced putting the images in my mind into paintings, as well as acting on them in my everyday life. I began to see myself as an artist. I had more courage to express myself, to live out what I learned from Argus. Rather than talk about it, I did it!

I took my first painting to a local gallery and it sold within the week. That was nine years ago. Since that time, I have had five one-person shows, won artistic awards, illustrated a book, and virtually made a living using my brushes and paints to express what I see and how I feel.

It has not happened all at once, nor has it been easy. I still have problems with old fears and anxieties around rejection, insecurities, fear of failure, and self-doubt, as I am sure we all do. Old verbiage still creeps into my head. "Who do you think you are, trying to make it as an artist? Everyone knows artists are crazy, and so are you!" Still, the image of Argus is always with me, showing me how to imagine and trust that dreams can and do come true.

Where dreams and wishes come true. . .

I have often envisioned myself dressed as Argus at a museum retrospective of my work. Argus is bowing and greeting the guests and blowing his kazoo. There would be "OOOH"s and "AHHH"s as he points out his favorite pieces. Perhaps there would be a life-sized self-portrait, much admired by himself, or a large still-life of his bright, shiny gold tennis shoes. What fun it would be! He would dance through the crowd and pose for the press. The ultimate art critic! What a story!

Is there a difference between interpretations and imaginations?

When we see a painting, it may mean something entirely different to us from what it means to anyone else. Is it wrong for each of us to have his/her own interpretation? When you were in school, did you always agree with the poetry interpretations given in class? We found ourselves giving the "correct" answers to get a good grade, yet wondering for years whose authority it was that gave those words that meaning.

Our school systems tend to diminish our capabilities to imagine by giving us too many instructions and only one "correct" answer. How can we avoid losing our precious child-like imaginations when we are constantly bombarded with so many rules, so many instructions, so many absolutes?

Have you ever listened to Harry Chapin's song, "Flowers Are Red"? We listen to it every time we put on our makeup. It reminds us of our uniqueness. It reminds us to respect the same in others. "There's no need to see flowers any other way than the way they always have been seen." We use our clowns to fight this sameness concept.

We see this concept reinforced regularly when we do school programs. We are conscious of the children being herded into the auditorium in preparation for a clown presentation, The children are young, first to third grade, excited and energetic. Their teachers are fiercely striving for control, and we hear the threats, "Don't get out of line!", "Be quiet!", "Don't you dare act up, or. . . ." Indeed, the struggle is not always just a verbal one. We sometimes wonder why children's arms don't grow so long they touch the ground, from being jerked around so much.

This struggle for "control" strikes us as so bizarre! Especially when one considers the entire scene. The stage is set with clown costumes and makeup and toys. Judy is greeting the children, encouraging them to sing with the music, "We Are the World." Pat is sitting on stage, swinging her legs, chewing gum and blowing bubbles.

Clowns are here to teach us that chaos is not always calamity. There are times when strict rules and order are not applicable nor necessary. It is our gift of imagination that allows us to know when to relax those rules. The children catch on fast, and have a wonderful time.

Labels express who we think we are
Symbols permit us to say who we are

III.

Symbols

Clowns transform the human form through paint, mime and costume. Clowns are playful and revive our inner magic to share with others. When we clown, we use a symbolic language which is an expression of the inner creative child.

The clown is a universal symbol which crosses all ethnic and time barriers. Clowns have been part of every culture's history. Perhaps clowns are like magnets, drawing us towards them from our inner desires to be child-like again. Children sense intuitively that clowns are trustworthy, clowns are fun, clowns are love.

With every image that comes to mind about "clown" we are aware of the energy fields that surround that picture. Clowns exude an enormous amount of energy. All bodies are created from energy. Our energy flows from the center, deep within us. Energy vibrates from people. We see this vibration, we feel it, but only when we are in our most awakened selves. When you are that energy, when you wear that energy (the symbol of the clown costume), you attract the same likeness in the other person. They are drawn irresistibly towards you—the Teacher, the Fool, the Healer, the Sage.

The white face of the clown symbolizes death. People applying the white face do so expecting to encounter the death of their egos. In doing this, we let go of inhibitions and fears that frequently prevent us from interacting with others. We let go of who we think we are or who we think we ought to be, and through the use of colors on our faces, create a vision of what IS.

Colors and designs on clown faces are all symbolic and have very special meaning to each person. Likewise, a clown's costume, colors and style are personal statements of individuality.

When we relate to others, we usually do so through our own veils. Our past experiences and expectations prejudice the way we relate, the way we listen, the way we comprehend.

Clowns, however, have no past and they have no future. They are always present in the moment, always living in the NOW. Thus they are able to communicate, to listen, to experience in a more open way. This we have learned through our clowning, and strive to carry through in our every day living, enriching our lives and the lives of those with whom we come in contact. When the clown is present, without veils of yesterday's garbage and tomorrow's shopping lists, he encourages others to respond with the same open-heartedness.

The clown has traditionally throughout centuries and cultures stood for many things—the Healer, the Teacher, the Sage, the Fool.

The Healer

The kid in all of us really wants to be intimate with everyone. A clown disarms people. Suddenly seeing a clown, whether you are driving to the mall in heavy traffic, or sick in a hospital bed, is such a shock to your system, it pushes you into a different frame of mind. Your first response is to want to be recognized, to smile, to shake a hand, to get a piece of bubble gum.

When we visit hospitals we are constantly faced with volumes of people wanting us to come into their rooms. "Hey clown, come in this room." Or someone will approach us hesitantly and request we visit a specific room.

There is growing acceptance in the medical community that laughter is good medicine. Emotions are key elements in battling illness, and laughter has been recognized as a healthy response, increasing endorphines, which are actually our body's natural pain relieving element. When people in intense pain are laughing, even for those few seconds, they have found relief from pain. It is this element we reach in people when we visit them in the hospital. For those few minutes when we are present to them, when they are smiling, the pain is eased and healing takes place. Notice we are not saying "curing," merely "healing," for those few minutes.

Magic in nursing homes? A parade of clowns skipping down the halls is therapeutic for both patients and staff. At the end of our day-long workshops on clowning for adults, after participants have discovered their clowns, and have applied makeup, donned costumes, and picked out toys or props, we announce that we are going on an adventure—to a nursing home! Amidst groans and complaints ("I hate nursing homes! They're so depressing!") we start our journey. Once inside, without exception, every person has been able to be loving and giving. They forget that it's a "depressing place" until the visit is over. Certainly none of them returned depressed, and they did not feel that way on the entire trip. Here is true evidence of transformation and loss of ego. It is the adult who is fearful of old age and dying. The clown/child passes through those barriers and is able to trust and embrace the aged in their suffering.

How often have we sat, caressing the hair of an aged woman in a wheel chair, listening to her stories, giving her our silent, unconditional love! Each person has been so remarkable. These old and lonely lives become vibrant and we as healers have been enriched.

Imagine Argus riding a red scooter and Blue racing to catch up. Imagine this happening on the hospice ward, for that is where we are—inviting people to give up their pain and sadness to play with us. And they do, again and again!

Our experience of living on the edge, in costume and in silence, has allowed us access to places and situations where we would otherwise be afraid to venture.

Years ago, Argus and Blue started clowning in hospitals. Hired by the chaplaincy office at a hospital, we would venture forth, visiting assigned patients. One of them was Dan.

We were asked to visit him because he was battling severe depression. Dan had had his second leg amputated because of diabetes complications. This was a serious blow to a man who was well known for his performances in local theater.

We approached his room timidly. He was surprised to see us, but welcomed us in. Now, as you may know, clowns have no sense of etiquette. We came in with our music and toys, but our first greeting to him was with gestures regarding the empty space in the bed where his legs should have been. We were puzzled by the emptiness, even going so far as to look under the bed and in the closet for what was missing. Responding to our frantic gestures, Dan told us about the operation. We gave him stickers, balloons, and wishes with our magic wand. Our greatest joy was when he finally responded to our requests for a song. We kept asking him to sing with our music, but he'd only reply, "I don't sing any more. You need to go to the children's hospital." Finally he relented to our coaxing, and sang "Hello, Dolly" in a deep, rich voice. We all had tears in our eyes. But we kissed him goodbye with the knowledge that his spirits had lifted.

The chaplain reported that Dan's physical and mental attitude had improved remarkably. Several days later, Pat happened to be near the hospital and dropped in for a visit.

She popped her head in the door and said, "Hi!" He smiled and responded. She started off, "You don't know me . . . ." But Dan replied, "Of course I know you. You're one of my clowns." Pat expressed her surprise, and Dan reminded her he was a theater person and could see beyond makeup. Dan inquired about our clowns and confided how touched he was by our attention. We talked about the obvious—the loss of his legs. Obvious to all, but other people who came to see him studiously avoided looking at the empty spot on the bed. Friends never mentioned the loss, perhaps from their own embarrassment. This was understandable, but it meant that no one gave him the opportunity to acknowledge his feelings or to express his loss—until the fools came to see him.

We did take Dan up on his suggestion and we also visited the children's hospital. Clowns are taken for granted by children. Perhaps they don't see it as anything special because THEY ALREADY BELIEVE IN MAGIC.

On one ordinary visit, however, we approached a boy in bed his leg in traction. We made a big deal over his cast, decorating it with many stickers. He joined us in a game of catch with a balloon. As soon as we started our routine he smiled and said, "Clowns, clowns. . ." Later we discovered this young boy had been in an automobile accident in which both parents had been killed. The boy had not spoken a word since the accident two weeks before our visit.

Clowns do perform magic! Just ask the children!

The Teacher

The Wise Old Chinese Teacher took his student to a cliff. They stood together at the edge, looking out into the mists and the distant valley far below. The teacher said to the student, "Jump." The student said, "Oh, Master, I

"My memories of love will be of you."

Argus at work #1.

The Sage

"Mirror, mirror, on the wall . . . ."

cannot do that, for I will kill myself." The Master said once again, "Jump." So the student stepped forward, placed his feet on the edge of the cliff, and leaped into space. He fell and fell and fell. And then. . .HE FLEW.

The way we teach is to be open to learning. We teach in such a manner that the conscious and unconscious mind can come together. There is no past, no future—only the moment at hand. It is during this time that both student and teacher often have the experience of "flying," for both are in the process of learning and teaching.

Teacher is also therapist. We jokingly started describing ourselves as "clown therapists," but have come to see that therapy actually does take place. The word "therapy" comes from the Latin *therapia,* meaning "to be an attendant." We see therapy as a service, we see ourselves as attendants to others. For we come with open hearts and a desire to be of service.

Can you remember having any teachers who were right all the time? More important, can you remember any teachers who were not afraid to be wrong some of the time, and not afraid to say so? We suspect that if you had such a teacher, he or she is still cherished in your memory. An unusual teacher indeed!

Anthony Jay, an executive in the film making firm, Video Arts Limited, has commented, "One can never forget something learned by laughing at someone doing it wrong." We feel that, as clowns, there is probably nothing we cannot teach.

Clowns teach in metaphors. We learn some very important lessons in our living in the very same way. Metaphors make pictures in our minds and allow us to create other options for ourselves. Pictures activate the right side of our brain, the instinctive, intuitive part. All of the "New Age" philosophies are making it more in vogue to use our right brain. But for most of us, we struggle to catch up. We want to use our creative and intuitive abilities. We need to get over our guilt for having used them in the past, when we were told we were wrong and foolish for doing so.

School systems, although they are more aware of individual differences than they used to be, are for the most part still ignoring children who are more right brain inclined. It is our fear that the intuitive and creative sides of our children will die of starvation and abuse in present-day school systems.

Now we are entering the computer age. If we come to depend on machines to do our communicating and calculating, this can lead to refusal to see each other or to really hear each other, further separating us and alienating us as human beings.

The clown builds bridges, uniting our left and right brain, acknowledging the necessity to learn mathematical equations precisely, yet allowing us to see the beauty of never ending changes in the colors of the rainbow.

A vital skit we perform while doing school programs is a mime to John Denver's song, "Perhaps Love." The end line, "The memory of love will be of you," is a statement of our relationship to one another, collectively, as a society of teachers and learners.

We choose our teachers, either consciously or subconsciously, all our adult lives. Our parents were our first teachers. We all know they made lots of mistakes, as their parents did, as we do. For everything our parents were (and were not), they were the first people to teach us.

In school, we were exposed to many teachers, people from various backgrounds—people who were happy and angry and sad. They all had a role in influencing our lives, and in some instances our very perceptions of who we are.

Professional teachers probably forget at times, as we all do, the impact we have on one another. The clown reminds us that teachers are present in many different forms. We teach in clown costume, but we also teach in clown spirit when we are not in "character."

The Fool

The clown is also represented by the Fool. It is that part that carries the magical quality of child-like belief and faith in the unknown.

In some Tarot cards the Fool is pictured as blindfolded, further emphasizing his ability to act by insight rather than eyesight, using intuitive wisdom instead of conventional logic. Blindfolding further symbolizes seeing with an inner eye. Many legends speak of blind prophets—prophets who do not see conventionally, but see what others cannot. Clowns do not see in a conventional manner, and are considered "foolish." Often we are so caught up in trying to make sense of everything, we miss the real meaning. Our need for explanations prevent us from seeing the mystery of life. The Fool believes in magic, and it is that belief that pulls him through.

Let's watch a scene from W.C. Field's film, *The Bank Dick* (1940). Fields drives a car at great speed while a bank robber in the seat behind him points a gun at him; they are chased by policemen on motorcycles. In the course of the pursuit, the controlling mechanisms of the car begin to disintegrate. Unperturbed, Fields throws away the gearshift and the brakes and passes the steering wheel to the robber. The car careens madly but without accident, dodging obstacles, until it finally comes to a halt at the very edge of a cliff. Fields steps out, the criminal having passed out with fright, to be greeted as a hero by the arriving police. "(That) the magical power that guides the car. . .belongs to the fool or. . .he belongs to it is shown by the fact that Fields takes the astonishing course of events completely for granted and that it ends in a triumph for him." (Willeford, William. *The Fool and His Scepter: A*

Study in Clowns and Jesters and Their Audience. Chicago: Northwestern University Press, 1969.)

There *is* magic in the air that surrounds the Fool. We laugh at his antics, we cry at his innocence, we rejoice in his victories.We have found that people are more open and less protective of their own vulnerabilities when they are in a safe environment, with a safe person. The clown as Fool can be such a person. He is not an authority figure, not an official—no white coat, no uniform, no big title. He is silent, there to listen, not to talk. Adults (kids too!) often open up readily to such a person. They trust the clown. They take him seriously. In return, we honor each person we encounter.

When we worked for the chaplain at the local hospital, we learned that the chaplain's father had died. The chaplain had done all the appropriate things—delivered the eulogy for his father, served the needs of his family. But what about his own grief, his own bereavement?

Argus decided that it was time for an appearance. He arrived at the chaplain's office with toy bag in hand and lots of extra Kleenex. He was ushered in by a much-surprised secretary and received by an equally-surprised chaplain. Argus gave a quick hug to the chaplain and proceeded to lay a small blanket and pillow on the nearby sofa. Motioning for him to lie down, Argus also handed him a teddy bear. Somewhat startled, the chaplain complied. Then Argus held up a small chalkboard with the word DAD written on it. As soon as Argus leaned back in an adjacent chair and propped his feet up, the chaplain began his story. He told of cherished childhood memories, his love for his father, and how much he missed him. The tears flowed as Argus hummed "Rock-A-Bye Baby" on his kazoo.

Here we can see the Child, the vulnerable Little One that resides in all of us. The Clown as Fool, who represents the child in all of us, can touch someone else's Child, so healing can take place.

The Fool will often exaggerate or appear absurd in order to make a point, touching some inner chord within us that results in some form of self-acknowledgment. Although it is at first humorous, we see ourselves much in the same way.

One of the most famous clowns in history had this ability. His name was Grock. Watch as he walks into the center ring of the circus, spotlights shining on him. The lights move to a piano sitting on one side of the ring. There is a piano stool on the opposite side. He walks over to the piano. Then, bending over painfully and making dramatic efforts, moaning and groaning, gasping for breath, he pushes the piano over to the stool. His feat accomplished, he begins to play.

How many times do we labor our way through life, forgetting that there may be a more simple way to accomplish a task or get what we need? How often we make things more difficult for ourselves by using old ways and patterns that no longer work for us, instead of looking for new choices that may work more effectively!

Grock is us. He brings us a sense of our own foolishness. Maybe, if we are lucky, he brings us the ability to laugh at ourselves as we push away at our pianos.

IV.

Communication

Words, written and spoken, are our major forms of communication. But so often, as the saying goes, "words fail us"—we cannot say what we want to say, and may even find that our words are setting up barriers to communication with other people.

Our clowns have taught us to communicate without words, for we have made a solemn promise not to speak once we have put on our makeup, no matter what happens. Therefore we speak by using body language or mime.

Silence is a language in and of itself. Around this theme we present programs at schools, often for children with learning disabilities. We speak to them about *big* words like COMMUNICATION, PANTOMIME, and TRANSFORMATION, and we teach many ways to talk to one another without using words. We ask them to "listen with your eyes, with your ears, and with your heart." One little boy asked what listening with your heart meant, and we replied that it is paying attention with a loving heart.

We take some time to tell them about what our clowns mean to us. Pat talks about how her clown loves to dress up and look pretty. She explains that we are not circus clowns, but magical clowns who visit schools and hospitals, sharing love. Pat holds up her costume, showing them her pink hair, pink overall suit, and pink polka-dotted shoes. She shows them the blue circle pin on the outfit and tells them she will want them to guess her name after she gets dressed.

Then Judy steps up and talks about Argus. She says Argus believes in rainbows and points to the rainbow ribbons on his shirt. She tells them Argus believes in Spring and beautiful flowers, and shows them his hat. Then she says that Argus believes in —"What's at the end of the rainbow?" Someone always pipes up, "Gold!" and Judy replies, "That's why Argus wears these wonderful gold tennis shoes!" Judy then tells the audience how much she appreciates people their age because being a clown keeps her in touch with the child inside of herself. Recently a youngster raised his hand and said, "That happened to my mother once and I ended up with a baby sister!"

During the next segment of the program, Pat talks about how our bodies can tell stories, and Judy stands behind her and mimics every move she makes. Of course, the children are laughing and Pat acts as though she doesn't know what is going on. Finally she understands. Then she tries to catch Judy in the act.

Now Pat informs the young audience that Judy is going to tell a story using her body. Judy places two chairs far apart in a straight line and she and Pat tie a rope between them, stretching it tightly. Judy raises her umbrella over her head—a sad object, for the fabric hangs from the spokes in tatters—and climbs onto one of the chairs. Pat motions to her to walk across the rope. The audience claps and cheers her on. Suddenly, Judy trembles with fear, makes a frightened face, and runs off to hide. Pat retrieves her, and brushes both Judy and the rope off with a feather duster. Then Pat encourages Judy to try again, telling her she *knows* she can do it.

Judy climbs on the chair, puts her foot out on the rope, pulls back, shakes her head, climbs down, and runs off again, making sobbing sounds. Pat grabs her, pulls her to the chair, urges her to try just one more time. Judy climbs onto the chair, and takes a couple of low bows. A mighty fanfare on the kazoo announces this final attempt to walk the tight rope.

Judy puts her foot out to test the rope—then jumps off the chair, pushes one chair closer to the other so the rope is touching the floor, and walks on the rope as if she has accomplished a real tight-rope performance. She bows to everyone for her grand finale. There are cheers and BOO's, and a few remarks—"She cheated!"—erupt from the crowd. Everyone laughs!

Pat steps up, motioning for quiet, and begins the next phase on Transformation. She tells the children that this word means "great change," like the change a butterfly undergoes. They will see a BIG change as Pat turns into Blue and Judy turns into Argus. Once more, they are reminded to watch and listen with their eyes, ears, and hearts.

We begin to put on our makeup as music plays in the background. Once the makeup is applied, we put on our costumes and ask some of the children to help us by buttoning our shirts or tying our shoes, because this age group has just learned how to dress themselves, and they enjoy using their new skills to help. At some point, Argus takes one of Blue's shoes and hides it, and Blue gets very sad at the loss of one of her precious polka-dotted tennis shoes. The children love to "tell on" Argus and help Blue find it. When she does, she usually blames the person who has it. She immediately puts her shoes on—but backwards! The children *very* quickly point out that she has her shoes on WRONG! When Argus dresses, he doesn't like to zip up his pants in front of everyone, so he turns his back to the audience and the children snicker at his embarrassment.

Finally we are dressed. We take a bow. Blue points to the round blue circle on her suspenders and tries to get the children to guess her name. There are responses of CIRCLE, ROUND, BLUE DOT, PINKY, and then someone gets it. BLUE! We all clap, bring the child up before the group, bow with the child, and give him a prize for

Argus at work #2.

guessing Blue's name. We motion for silence—hands over our mouths. All is quiet and music begins to play. Argus and Blue do a mime to John Denver's "Perhaps Love."

When it is over we walk to the exits. Teachers and children file by to receive balloons and hugs and kisses.

In watching, in experiencing, this form of communication, children and teachers alike are transformed. They watch, sometimes as many as 80 in a group, in silence and compatibility, mesmerized by their own altered consciousness.

Following one such program, a boy approached Blue. He put his head on her chest, then he looked deeply into her eyes and smiled. He hugged her for a long time. Then he ran over to Argus and hugged him. The teachers' voices were heard in the background. "Look, he's hugging the clowns," they exclaimed in amazement. We made a parade returning to the classroom, the boy holding hands with both clowns, skipping down the hall. When we arrived at his classroom, he went to a pallet on the floor, and crawled onto it, curling up like a small baby, facing the wall. We later learned from the teachers that he had *never* responded to any stimulation in such a manner. The boy was autistic. Are there words for this?

Because we did not speak, he spoke! To us, this is nothing short of a miracle.

A Story

(This is part of chapter on communication, but it seems to be about imagination and symbols and creativity, too.)

The chaplain's office called again. Judy donned her clown attire. She was to meet Pat/Blue at the hospital. Along the way, she waved at all the depressed people in their cars and beeped at people on the highway. But, as she turned a curve, a loud noise knocked from the car. Argus jumped from the car (remembering to stop it first!), ran around the car, looked under the car, but refused to look under the hood for fear of what would be found. Besides, Argus wouldn't know what was under the hood anyway. So he returned to the driver's seat and slowly moved to the nearest gas station. The loud knocking sound got louder. As he entered the gas station, the attendant came striding forth with hands uplifted. "STOP!" Argus stepped from the car just in time to see that the left front wheel was ready to fall from the axle. He got down on hands and knees and begged the attendant to let the car remain there until he figured it all out. Same answer, "NO!" Argus stood there for a moment, walked into the office, and wrote on a sheet of paper that he was going down the street to AAA. The attendant gave a begrudging, "Okay, but hurry." Off Argus ran down the street to the office of AAA. Panting and gasping, he was confronted with many people standing in several lines. What to do? Suddenly, he raced to the front of the line and slammed his large toy bag down on the counter and let out a loud cry. A clerk appeared and said, "Excuse me, is your car disabled?" Argus made a frantic nodding motion. "Well, come this way. I'm sure we will be able to help you." Argus skipped into the manager's office behind the woman. Everyone turned to look at the latest customer in distress. A secretary sat behind a desk talking on the phone. "Harold, you won't believe what just walked into the office." With that, she described Argus from head to foot and hung up the phone. The manager refused to help, but the secretary took full charge. "Have you brought your AAA card?" Argus shook his head—typical clown, he had left it at home. "Well, write down your name and address and we'll locate your identification number." She returned in a few minutes with the correct information and reported that a cab had been called and would be around in a few minutes, and that a tow truck would move the car to another gas station. Argus jumped up and down and gratefully passed out bubble gum to all the employees. He ran outside to wait for the cab. He began to wave to all the cars and buses when he heard a voice behind him. He turned around to see a little old lady sitting on a bench. "Are you a clown?" He shook his head no and ran to the front of the AAA building. A man walked out and Argus ran to him and stuck out his thumb to tell him he really needed a ride. The man smiled and said, "Sure, where are you going?" Argus motioned towards the hospital, grabbed his neck and made gagging sounds as if he were sick. "Oh, to the hospital?" Argus nodded yes. On the ride to the hospital, the man begged Argus to visit his wife, who was sick in another hospital. They pulled up at their destination. Argus shook the man's hand, gave him a paper heart, blew him a kiss, and dashed into the hospital to find Blue.

Meanwhile, back at the ranch (the ladies' room at the hospital where they were supposed to meet), Blue had overcome the panic of worry about Argus.

Blue spent the first half-hour pacing, even practicing facial expressions and routines in the mirror when she was alone. Every time the door would open, she would perk up and smile, give out balloons and bubble gum. It became evident to her that a good many of the women coming into the ladies' room had other things on their minds besides the usual pressing physical necessities. There was real pain in their eyes and it seemed to Blue that they were coming in to escape distress, if only for a moment.

Obviously, most people do not expect to confront a clown when they enter the ladies' room, but Blue found herself responding to more than the surprised expressions. She began to respond to their eyes, and intuitively to their hearts. Thus, she laughingly distributed gum and hugs with some. But with others, she reached into her pocket and produced a huge handkerchief (pink, of course!), offered to dry tears, and lent her shoulder for comfort. When she saw how people responded and thanked her, with a comment, "I sure feel better now, but no one will believe this," her heart was filled with joy.

After all this, when Argus walked through the door, she was totally relieved to see him. They hugged and were happy to start new adventures.

Blue later reported to the medical authorities that clowns should be placed in every rest room in the hospital to hear people's stories, for that is where many go to shed their tears. It would be a perfect opportunity for healing.

V.

You As Clown

How do ordinary people take that leap from security into the unknown? Why should you risk entering the center ring of your life?

It is our belief that there comes a time when we need to explore different avenues for personal growth. For us, clowning has been one of those avenues.

All of us search for ways to provide safe and secure lives for ourselves. Much childhood learning, at home and at school, is devoted to how to accomplish this. Yet as adults, we may find ourselves following these carefully-learned rules and regulations and suddenly discovering that they don't work. Or we feel stuck and unable to find our way, unable to go to a seemingly obvious next step, such as finding a new partner or changing our lives in order to live more fully.

The clown helps us take the risks and try the fresh approaches which give us new experiences. Our clowns give us the opportunity to express ourselves differently.

Different: Often we ask ourselves what makes us so different? Argus and Blue are not typical clowns. We remember clown conferences we have attended. Everyone else was having such a great time, but we found many of the speakers boring, and had a sense of not belonging. Finally we came to the conclusion that our motives for being clowns have always been different. Some people have taken our workshops and have gone on to become wonderful entertainers. Freebee is a great magician, performing in silence, and Lollipop is a terrific hit with children at birthday parties. But our motivation was always different. From the onset, we viewed the clown as a teacher. We investigated the art of clowning because of a vision. With no expectations, and no idea of where we were going, we followed a dream and lived it.

Spotlight on the Center Ring again! Enter the clown—you the reader, transformed! Envision yourself as clown, entering the center ring of the circus. Have the courage to allow yourself the luxury of living in the "don't know"—just for this moment, not to need the answers to "How?" or "Why?" Just to BE. Trust, for this moment, your own creativity, your own imagination, and step off the edge with us to find your own symbols. When we live for this moment, when we face our fears for just this moment, our "moments" start to expand. "Just for this moment" becomes, not a minute nor an hour, but an entire lifetime.

But for right now, for just this moment, see a magic wand appear before you, sprinkling you with star dust and wonder. We extend to you another invitation, to create your own clown.

Allow your mind to take a great adventure, a treasure hunt through visualizations seeking symbols of your clown. Finding a quiet space, ask yourself these questions. These questions have only your own personal answers, and you are invited to respond with images. Answer not with words, but pictures in your mind. It would be helpful to have paper and crayons or colored pencils handy.

When you were small:
What was most embarrassing to you?
What was the most fun thing you did?
What was your favorite chair?
With whom did you sit?
What were your favorite games?
What were your favorite colors?

Give your mind the time and patience to explore answers. Look at the images you have created and see what blends. You may develop other questions, or create other pictures. Put them together. Look for similarities in your pictures, symbols or colors that are meaningful to you. Perhaps you have never realized some things that were important to you. Use these symbols for your clown. Take these images/pictures in your mind, and find something in the real world to represent that and give it form. For instance, if your most fun thing to do is to go fishing, your clown may wear oversized fish waders or large overalls and boots, perhaps fish hooks dangling from a hat. Nurse Goodbody, fulfilling an unattainable fantasy, wears a white uniform, huge nursing cap, and gigantic you-know-whats. In fact, she can hardly find her stethoscope between the you-know-whats!

This important exercise of asking the subconscious for pictures and putting them into tangible reality is one of many in our all-day workshops, which were designed not only from our experiences, but for the fun of it!

Come Clownin' with me
Come Clownin' with me
In the moonlight
Come Clownin' with me

Workshops

Each of us needs tools and visions for growth. For us and for participants in our workshops, the clown has been that tool—the vehicle that permits us to balance our dreams with our realities.

Imagine enrolling in a clown workshop, your first! Feel the nervous energy in the pit of your stomach. It feels something like excitement, but behind it also you hear that nagging voice, "What if someone finds out I'm doing something so foolish?" For whatever reason, you show up, carrying a silly hat, a noisemaker, and your lunch. You are ready for a fun-filled day, and God knows what else! You are faced with a large sign at the door, "ENTER YOUR LIGHTER SIDE."

Taking a deep breath and hoping your lighter side is showing, you enter a room filled with music and ten other people looking just as nervous as you! Pat and Judy invite each of you to write your name on a heart name tag, and join them in a circle sitting on the floor. The room is carpeted, and one side is lined with mirrors and makeup. Another corner looks interesting. There is a brass trunk with costumes hanging out of it, and toys all around.

During introductions, you are given a small sparkling heart sticker to put on the person next to you. Already you are learning to give your heart away. Judy and Pat talk about their clowns and what clowning means to them, and you find yourself relaxing. You talk about the hat you brought and listen to the stories of your new counterparts in clowning. Next you try expressing how the hat makes you feel. You laugh in amazement as people walk, jump, and perform various gyrations to describe without words how their hats make them feel.

Now it is time to look at emotions. Clowns, you are told, express what they are feeling with their faces and bodies. How long have you held on to emotions, secreting

Magic happens only when you believe in it.

them away, not giving yourself permission to express or even to feel them? You walk in a circle with everyone else. Someone calls out an emotion—"Joy." People hop and skip and laugh. "Sadness"—people exaggerate crying, weeping, slow movements. "Anger"—it becomes difficult not to laugh at the antics. How good it feels to be expressive in such a light atmosphere! Then you grab a partner and practice making funny faces and imitating one another. You are rapidly learning there are no strangers in this group—or maybe you're learning that everyone in the group is strange!

Pat announces it is time to play games. How long has it been since you've played? Not games to win or lose, not to challenge or threaten, just games for pure fun!

The first game is musical chairs. Chairs are lined up and Judy monitors the music. You are dismayed when the music stops and you are the first one without a seat—until you find out about the new rule. Pat takes away a chair, but everyone still plays, you just find a lap to sit on. The game progresses, chairs disappear, laps become overloaded, laughter is uproarious.

When the laughter calms down, everyone puts their chairs in a circle for another game, "Pass the ball." A large ball is placed in someone's lap. The instructions are simple. Just pass the ball around the circle. As the ball starts on its first round, Judy remembers the other rule, "I almost forgot—you can't use your hands." This is still not too difficult a challenge and most of you manage to get the ball to the person next to you. Then someone drops the ball, but Judy is there to help. She picks up the ball, and drops a baseball into the person's lap instead. This calls for a little more ingenuity, but you all manage with a little practice. But then—oh no—Judy jumps up to "help" again—this time substituting a golf ball.

These two games have given the child in you ample time to emerge. You are not even aware that your consciousness has changed, but you realize how playful you are. Do you wonder how long it has been since you've felt that way? Or why you permitted yourself to "grow up"?

Pat and Judy are now pantomiming. You sit again with your cohorts watching them struggle with a large invisible box. Pat explains that this is their toy box. One person comes up, picks a toy from the box, plays with it, gives it to someone else. That person plays with it, returns it to the box, and gets another toy. You all have a turn. Imagination is now in high kilter as the toy box yields tops, dolls, wagons, bikes, yoyos, even bubble gum.

The announcement of lunch time comes as a surprise. In all the commotion, your stomach never did remind you of the time. Everyone brings out a lunch bag. You are not surprised by this time when Pat brings out her ET lunch box that has seen better days. Lunch is carefree—discussions of the morning activities, getting to know one another. Judy produces a huge bag of Tootsie Rolls to share. You wonder, "Is it only kids who get hyper on too much sugar?"

People quiet down and start cleaning up. A tape of soft harp music is put on, and everyone gathers in a circle. You all lie on the floor, feet in the center, like spokes in a wheel. The sense of connected-ness is solid. It is time to explore a new adventure. You are about to head into your subconscious, seeking your clown.

Lights are dimmed, music plays, and by candlelight Pat reads a reverie. The reverie, or guided imagination, is designed to assist you in visualizing your clown.

> Today we are going to take a trip to the beach. We are going to use our imagination, that part of our mind that sees pictures and can create anything we wish. In preparation for the trip, quietly and slowly take three or four deep breaths. Breathe so quietly that no one can hear it. Hold your breath for a moment

and slowly release it. As you do this, be aware of your body becoming quiet and still and your mind becoming quiet and alert.

Now lift your thoughts to that place of imagination and make-believe. Visualize yourself on a beautiful beach. The sun is warm and gentle. The cool sea breeze blows gently on you. The weather is perfect. Lie down and feel the gentle warmth of the sand beneath you. Close your eyes and listen to the sound of the ocean waves breaking and rolling in a quiet rhythm. . .Hear the cry of seagulls and watch them flying lazily in the blue sky. . . . You feel good, at peace. Lie there looking at the white fluffy clouds, the seagulls. . . .Smell the fresh salt air. . . .Listen to the ocean. . . Feel the warm sand. All is good and you feel very safe.

Become aware of carousel music far down the beach. Get up and walk towards the sound. There before your very eyes are clowns. . .doing cartwheels, somersaults, standing on their heads. . . all playing on the beach. One comes up to you and motions for you to come and join the group. Another clown comes up to you. He has on a bright blue wig and shows you his clown watch that plays "Yankee Doodle Dandy" on the hour, every hour. Then all the clowns gather to show you their tricks. They dance and pull you into dancing in the circle of clowns. . . whirling and whirring to the carousel music. Dance with them. . .be a part of them. As you turn, you see a clown with stringy orange hair smile at you with his huge red grin. He has beautiful, brightly-colored balls which he juggles into the air and suddenly, one drops into a pool of water between you. You dive into the water, reaching out to touch the beautiful ball. It goes up towards the surface of the water. As you reach for it, your head surfaces above the water and you see a wondrous old clown with white hair. His white clown suit is sprinkled with gold stars. Blue ruffles surround his neck and shoulders and wrists.

> He motions for you to come forward. You climb from the water and sit before the Old Clown. He smiles at you through twinkling turquoise eyes. You sit before him and he speaks.
>
> "This ball is the magic ball that you seek. In it, you will find the message of the heart and the power to cut loose those things that limit you and prevent you from finding yourself. You will discover the clown that lives in you and you will find that everything is possible in the 'Land of Make-Believe,' the place where your path has no end."
>
> Then he tosses the glass ball into the pool. You dive after it once again. It is floating just ahead of you. Just as your fingers grasp it, you hear the ocean waves and you open your eyes to see the blue sky, the sea-gulls flying overhead. You are awake. . .you are lying on the sandy beach.

The bodies next to you begin to stir. You gradually become aware, with some amazement, that the surface beneath you is not warm sand, but the hard floor. Stiffening muscles start to complain, and you sit up and rub a tender knee. The atmosphere in the room is one of quiet awe. Slowly, people begin sharing their experiences. Visions of vivid colors, senses of smell and touch awakening. . .As each shares, you realize this has been a unique adventure for all of you. One person is concerned that she had trouble envisioning anything. Pat assures her that often this reverie must be practiced for any results, especially if people are not accustomed to any form of meditation.

Keeping in mind the colors and perhaps costumes you saw in your guided reverie, you approach the mirrors with skeptical reluctance. Judy is excited, talking about different colors that can be used and urging everyone to grab a space at the mirrors. You are shown how to apply the baby oil and then the white face. The heavy and sticky feeling of the white makeup in the palm of your hand makes you hesitate. Your rational mind tells you, "It's not too late to run." Your eyes meet those of the person next to you. As you grin sheepishly at one another, you instinctively know he was thinking the same thing. You each take a deep breath, and with an internal "Okay, Fool," you begin to transfer the white mess to your face.

It is done. Judy makes a few minor repairs to smooth over some wrinkles. Look with astonishment at the results of the empty white mask reflecting back at you. You joke for a few minutes with your friends, who all look the same as you. With no further reluctance or fear you reach for the colors. A new sense of self confidence fills your heart as you view your own transformation. Again with some help from Judy your colors are set in place. By now most people are crowding around the brass trunk, grabbing pants and shirts, colorful scarves and dresses. Without exception all hesitancy has disappeared. It's a mass game of dress up!

As you stand, holding hands with all your new friends, you understand why Pat and Judy have been insisting all day in their faith in Magic. The magic has transformed you all. It is an experience you will never forget.

Masks—The White Face of the Fool

When we were growing up, we took part in the annual adventure of Halloween. This meant some time spent in deciding what our costumes would be and wondering how much candy we could get from the neighbors. One of the most important features of the character and costume was the mask. Somehow, it was wearing the mask that empowered us to be the character which was, perhaps, some hidden part of ourselves.

We use the same principle when we wear the white face mask of the clown. We have often been asked if our clown faces were our real faces. We always reply that they are.

Each of us wears many masks in everyday life. These masks are what we present to society. Strangely, when wearing the "persona" of white face, the essence, the "real" person, comes forth. White face is not something to hide behind, but more like something to feel safe *in*. Wearing white face enables us to let out previously unexpressed emotions, frees up our actions, helps us be more expressive. We become our truest selves.

While applying makeup before an audience, we become aware of the hush, the sense of anticipation and the absolute attention of those present. We begin by removing our every day makeup. This makes us feel exposed and vulnerable. We pin our hair and begin to apply the thick white cream to our faces. Then Argus powders Blue's face, causing her to cough and sneeze loudly, and Blue turns "blue" from holding her breath for so long.

Although we begin to be more playful while applying the makeup, we find this time to be totally focused and involved. There is an air of awe surrounding this event. Once the make up and costume are complete, we are relating with ourselves, one another, and the group in a different capacity. It is a time that feels sacred—as if we are children again, anticipating Christmas or our birthdays. We no longer feel fearful over what is to come. We experience excitement—as if something wonderful and beautiful is about to happen. The excitement becomes an expectation and it is at this point we *become* the clown. We expect and hope for something good to come about, and it usually does! If it does not, our masks remind us of the opportunity to change the situation or even our minds.

I.D.

It's a bright sunny day. Argus and Blue skip into a local hospital and are immediately met by a very official, rather large nurse who asks, "Where did you come from and who sent you?" Argus and Blue look at one another, fumble in their pockets for their wallets, shrug their shoulders, make grimacing faces to show how scared they are, and then point to heaven. Blue gives the nurse a hug, Argus hands her a Love balloon. Permission has been granted and off they go to explore the hospital and see what new adventure awaits them.

Costumes

As a child, one of my favorite games was "Dress-Up." I can't imagine a child who hasn't sneaked into Mom's or Dad's closet to try on a jacket, a dress, or a pair of heels.

I remember my friends and I collected all sorts of old clothes and gowns and played dress-up every day. The world of Make Believe could change daily, or even several times a day. Ah, the satisfaction of making a loud and visible statement!

Of course, we all grew up (most of us) (well, most of the time). We started choosing our own daily costumes, as it were. From the time we first started exercising our independence by refusing to wear what Momma put out for us, we started to choose our own statements of who we were becoming. Look around at what we've become—lawyers in business suits, doctors in white jackets, artists in bright colors, slobs in mismatched clothes, clowns in costumes. Our roles are so rigid. Costumes allow us to soften those boundaries.

In our daily statements of who we are, does it ever occur to most of us to put on something different?—maybe just to change the pace or mood. What a freeing experience when we become our clowns, putting on the costumes, completing the statement of form: THE CLOWN.

For each clown the costume is uniquely expressive of his or her personality. Blue, who loves her pink Nikes and lace gloves, starts coming alive every time Pat takes the pink overalls out of the closet.

Perhaps the costume is actually the safety net. Once the makeup is set, donning the costume is the final act of transformation. It gives us permission to go into even the most unlikely places.

We took an entire group of our new clowns to a wonderful old home and museum that sits on a river's edge. With total expectation of acceptance we presented ourselves at the door. We were met with surprise, yet our offering of bubble gum and balloons was taken as admission fee. With delight one of the guides gave us a "first class" tour.

I can just see Judy going up to an admission booth, plopping down a pile of gum and expecting to be let in. I can just see Judy being escorted out by security guards. Yet, Argus in full costume has no problem!

It is the making of the total clown that completes the symbols. Clowns in full costume act like they belong, so they do! If we act like it, we believe in it. Is it now so?

Changing our perception of reality directly affects what happens to us, which is an important lesson for us all to learn even if it means "dressing-up."

Another Story

One day Argus and Blue took a group of their "baby" clowns to play with the patients at the hospital. They were to observe their own feelings and how other people reacted to them as clowns. They came to an elevator and everyone piled into it. Everyone but Argus, that is. The

"Smile! You're on wooden camera!?"

doors closed and left Argus standing all alone and separated from the group. He frantically pushed the UP button and paced the floor until the next elevator arrived. Once on the elevator, he pushed all the buttons so he could check the floors, hoping he would find his friends. The elevator hit several floors and Blue and the others were not to be found. Finally, he picked a floor, thinking they would be there. He saw several people behind a glass window sitting at a table and he walked in and sat down. He made several "whew" sounds and mopped his brow with a napkin. He noticed several trays with plates and left-over food. A young girl sat nearby. She looked a little lonely, so Argus pushed a piece of bubble gum her way. She said they weren't allowed to have anything to eat that wasn't prescribed by the doctors. Argus made a gagging motion with his finger. The girl said, "That's right, it'll make us sick." Argus made gagging sounds and rubbed his tummy. With that the girl proceeded to tell him why she was in the hospital. All she did was throw up! After listening to her story, Argus blew her kisses and ran out into the hall—to discover he was on the eating disorders unit.

Props

Every clown will tell you that his props are his life's blood. For some it is magic tricks, others have their own special gimmicks, some tell jokes or do balloon sculptures.

Most of our props are carried in a large red bag. Of course Argus has to carry it because it doesn't match Blue's outfit. When relating to an individual, we trust the magic, and pull out just the right toy to facilitate communication. From a wooden camera (Argus loves to take pictures) to a rubber chicken (always reliable for a laugh) to a large paper heart (for the dearest of people)—we've got something for everyone.

Since hearts are our trademark, we have an abundance of red heart stickers which we plaster everywhere we go—on patients, wheelchairs, casts, and doctors' lapels. We use our kazoos to announce our arrival, and a bicycle horn to get people out of our way. Blue has a special interest in animal puppets and has quite a collection. She brings them to children's hospitals and nursing homes. Children and the elderly are particularly attracted to the animals which move realistically. They pet the animals and talk to them. It provides an opportunity for them to express affection. Sometimes it is painfully obvious that it is the first chance they've had in a long time for such an expression.

We're always on the lookout for spontaneous props. These items seem to pop up on just the right occasions. Gurneys and wheelchairs are ideal. Blue loves to hitchhike a ride whenever she can. In most instances an attendant is just as open to play when he's wheeling an empty chair down a corridor, and sees a clown with her thumb out.

A ringing telephone is great for a mime, but let's not forget the most obvious—elevators! Blue loves elevators with mirrors. Argus loves to ride on them and stop at every floor, sometimes more than once.

We use props to trigger other people's imaginations. As we do this, the props enhance our own, and we in turn, coming full circle, enhance others'.

Imagery

If we continuously lock ourselves into daily ruts, and do not take the time to nurture our inner selves, we stifle our creative powers and lose our visions. Imagery is a means for unlocking our inner doors and allowing our dreams to come true.

Imagery has many forms—dance, skits, art, journaling, guided visualizations. We can use all of these in exploring our inner clowns.

Participants in our workshops are introduced to guided imagery as a tool for exploration for their inner clowns. They are encouraged to use this means for future guidance. Those who can remember having imaginary playmates can understand this. Memories are shared about talking and playing, even naming an imaginary friend who gave companionship and advice. Going into guided meditation is like holding hands with that friend again, and racing towards a new adventure.

You may remember from an earlier chapter that we use non-threatening and specific scenarios as the guide. We do this to assist those who are not accustomed to any meditation. It helps them see the pictures of their mind's eye. We also do this to create a safe place. Often people fear journeying into the subconscious, especially if much pain is buried there.

Our friend Marilyn comes to mind. Marilyn took our workshop with several trusted friends from her Adult Children of Alcoholics group. She came with a wonderful hat, a gregarious sense of humor, and definite goals in mind of how she wanted to use her clown. The morning was exciting and Marilyn contributed great vitality to the skits. When we started preparing for the imagery part, she froze. The group listened compassionately as she tearfully described her fears. She had been troubled for years with recurring nightmares and frightening visions. The thought of undergoing a guided dream was understandably terrifying. We explored options. Sensing the magnitude of the situation, we suggested she go outside, maybe to the 7-11 for a soda. Another suggestion was for her to sit in a chair and listen to the guided imagery, participating if she chose, with open eyes, knowing that she had the group's permission to leave if she needed to do so. We all waited in loving silence while Marilyn, with downcast eyes, considered the options. Finally, taking a deep breath, Marilyn announced her choice—a third option. "I know you all love me. I want to share what you are experiencing. It is time to step out of my fear. I want to try it. If two people will hold my hands so I know I'm not alone, I'll try."

We all had tears in our eyes as we assured Marilyn of our love and support. It was unanimously agreed that we would undertake the imagery together, and that it was okay to stop if it got scary. The lights were left on and Pat started the reading, mindful of the terror Marilyn might express.

As the reading progressed, Marilyn's grip on her friends' hands relaxed. Her entire body visibly softened. The sharing afterwards was an incredible experience for us all. We cried with Marilyn over her description of beautiful colors and her sense of finding a peaceful and safe place after all the years of fright.

Marilyn's clown emerged with glory. We all celebrated her miracle of transformation. Marilyn is still clowning, using her clown character with other friends as liturgical clowns.

Life is **SHORT**

VI.

Self-Confidence

Self-confidence is often elusive for us. It flies in and out of our lives like a butterfly.

Some of us are led to believe by our life experiences that we can't do much, that our lives have no value, and perhaps that life itself is not very interesting or worthwhile. The clown revises these experiences, gives us permission to see ourselves as really belonging in this world. As we begin to see that it is a gift to be here even for this short minute, this short while, we experience the true beauty of being alive.

When teaching our workshops, we often marvel at how creative people are and how quickly they recognize their ability to be playful and imaginative. The old messages of lacking and not being good enough begin to lose their power, and words like MORE and BEAUTIFUL become more prominent in their vocabularies.

Clowning gives us new ways to see and believe in ourselves. If we have enough courage to walk into some unknown and scary place, we learn very quickly that we can accomplish things that we never thought possible.

A part of self-confidence is learning how to be gentle with yourself, and yet laugh at yourself at the same time. We have seen some people really *try* to become clowns. They spend hours and hours on their costumes, striving to have all the proper gear. Their serious effort is painful to watch, and the humor gets lost.

Inner growth evolves. Even with great effort, it cannot be forced. Do you have problems because you see yourselves on a time table for achievement of your dreams?

An ancient story is helpful in bringing this point into clearer focus. There is a Zen story which offers advice on achieving that delicate balance between disciplining ourselves and letting go.

> A young boy traveled across Japan to the school of a famous karate artist. When he arrived he was given audience with the master.
>
> "What do you want from me?" the master asked.
>
> "I wish to be your student and become the finest karateka in the land," the boy replied. "How long must I study?"
>
> "At least ten years," the master answered.
>
> "Ten years is a long time," said the boy. "What if I studied twice as hard as all your other students?"
>
> "Twenty years," replied the master.
>
> Becoming discouraged, the boy again asked, "Surely not twenty years! What if I practice day and night with all my effort?"
>
> "Thirty years."
>
> "How is it that each time I say I will work harder, you tell me that it will take longer?" the boy asked.
>
> The master replied, "The answer is clear. When one eye is fixed upon your destination, there is only one eye left with which to find the way."

Having fun and even being silly lightens our spirits, and helps us to forget the anxieties of finding our way. It is important to put both head and heart together. We believe that the great human GUFFAW works miracles in building the bridge between thinking and feeling. Journeying through life with your clown, or as clown, is one way to be good to yourself.

We remember one of our workshop participants. Mike was a quiet, shy man. Slight of build, he took obvious pride in his tattoos and talked of his love for being in the Marine Corps. During sharing times throughout the day, he was unwilling to interact with other participants, even though he took the workshop with several acquaintances.

During lunch break we quietly discussed our concern that he was not getting anything out of the day.

After lunch we had a scarf dance. Each person is given a brightly- colored scarf, and encouraged to interact with the music and other people's energy fields. It is a beautiful sight. The room is darkened, with only a candle casting shadows. Colors from scarves blend as dancers lose themselves in the music. It was during this dance that Mike started experiencing transformation. Sometime during those brief moments of losing his self-consciousness he found his self-confidence.

After the dance, it was time to put on makeup. Mike chose a simple face, accenting his eyes as stars. Then he put on a large shirt and pants with rainbow suspenders that had silly sayings on them. To top it off, he donned a black derby hat. He stood in front of the mirror, mesmerized by his reflection. He let out a soft, slow whistle, and whispered, "Wow, ain't I somethin'?" He was beautiful and he knew it! When everyone was ready, we piled into a van and headed for a nursing home. He did not need our extra concern any more. He acted like a pro! At the end of the day, tired but ecstatic, he kept his face on and we gave him the colored scarf, the symbol of his newly found self-confidence.

I once said to you
or
You once said to me
It's not attaining the goal
or
Grabbing the riches
It's the adventure of the

Journey.

VII.

Intuition

Visionaries and prophets have always relied on a higher sense of being. They have used intuition as the key for unlocking the subconscious. Using intuition in a healthy way keeps us open, alive, and creative.

Intuition is a sense of "knowing," a second sight which enables us to function more wholly as individuals. It is often difficult to trust this basic instinct. Inner voices mock us with, "What will they think?" "What if I lose?" "How safe will it be?" As these inner voices of fear grow louder, the fear of failure becomes deeper.

When you are in full clown costume and unable to talk, you become more aware of your own inner imagery, which is often drowned out by the sound of your voice. You become more in tune with the pictures in your mind and you begin to put these pictures into action.

Often, while clowning, we have experienced a "seventh sense" which helps us to know what the appropriate action is. This sense often kicks in under adverse circumstances. As we learn to trust this "knowing" we become more comfortable putting it into practice, both in and out of clown character.

As children we trusted what we were told as well as what we felt. But as we grew up we learned to suppress the ability to trust. Disappointments and cynicism were cruel teachers. They taught us that people do sometimes lie and we began to suspect that our feelings, as well, lied.

The rational mind clings to the desire to be right. It demands assurance. Whenever we are faced with making decisions we want to know that we are doing it right. Somehow, in some way, from someone, we want a written guarantee. And we call that timid thing a rational mind! Curious, when we really know that there are no guarantees and risks abound in every avenue of our lives.

Trust. It should be a major word in our vocabularies.

Trust also implies risk, because when we act on our "gut feeling" other people may not understand. Feelings can be unexplainable. It can be difficult to say, "I'm doing this because it feels like it's the best thing to do," especially when we expect acceptance from someone else.

Now, you may ask, what does clowning have to do with all this?

The answer lies in another story. One of our clown participants had just completed one of our workshops. We were clowning around at a shopping mall and park area. Our new clown friend had to leave us before we had completed the "play time," and later called Judy to relay an incident that had occurred as she was leaving the park.

Chloe was skipping along playing her kazoo. As she approached a park bench, she saw a man sitting there scowling at her. When she was in front of him, he stuck his foot out and tripped her, causing her to fall and scrape her knee—a knee that had given her years of trouble, having been operated on several times. She began to make crying sounds and the man laughed. Finally, she was able to get up and hobble over to where the man sat. She looked at him with great tenderness and handed him a "LOVE" balloon.

When we look at this story out of clown character, we fantasize many different scenarios of what we could have done to this man, from screaming at him, to kicking him in the shins, to calling the police. We ponder what type of person could be so mean, and we wonder if he had any notion or concern about the real physical pain he caused.

Yet in the moment, with an open heart, the clown, although injured, responded with love. It was her first impulse, her sense of intuition that this was a person in desperate need of unconditional love. Later, with knee elevated in an ice pack, she could enjoy the luxury of what she would have liked to have done to him. Only in the state of mind in which we clown was Chloe able to touch him with such compassion.

Group Therapy??

Argus was invited to a therapy group by a therapist whose clients were *very* shy. The clients knew that someone special was coming, but did not expect a clown!

The evening arrived and Argus knocked on the door where the group was meeting. When the door opened, he looked in for a minute, then turned and ran down the hall. He got up his courage once again and knocked on the door. The door opened and off he went again—down the hall and under a desk. After a few minutes, he came out of hiding and tried once more to join the group. This time, when he knocked on the door, the person who answered grabbed Argus, pulled him inside, and ushered him to a vacant seat. He sat down, everyone welcomed him with a round of applause, but he sat with his face hidden in his hands. Someone said, "Are you shy?" Argus nodded his head, yes, he was. Slowly, he peeked out from behind his hands and smiled. The group cheered!

Argus stood up and began to get acquainted with the people by opening his red toy bag and passing out his toys, including a rubber chicken. There were warm smiles and lots of laughter. Argus found a large white, fur boa and draped it around a beautiful woman's neck. She waltzed around the room as if she were a glamorous movie star! Then Argus turned on music and everyone played the musical chair game where everyone wins.

Each time the music stops one chair disappears, but all the players still remain in the game. After several rounds, the result is a large "people pile" in the one remaining chair.

When the games slowed down, one of the men did too. He flopped into a chair and reported that his work load had increased and he was just too tired to do anything. So Argus sat the weary man in his lap and hummed "Rock A Bye Baby" as the man cried and cried. The group told him it was all right to cry, and each member of the group came to him and gently patted him until it was over.

Then it was time to go. Argus turned on his music box and the tune "Impossible Dream" drifted around the room as Argus gathered his toys, passed out LOVE balloons and hugged all the members of the group before leaving. He waved them a goodbye and the door softly shut.

Later the therapist told Argus that everyone in the group thought Argus *knew* them—knew who they were.

A Dream

Let a clown into your life, and all kinds of things happen.

The power of the Fool casts light into many shadowed places.

This dream transpired following a discussion with a friend who was attending a feminist creative writing class. She spoke about women's anger and pain—the patriarchy and men's needs to suppress women. I suddenly saw that men must be suffering too, and a wide gap was forming between the sexes. I began to formulate questions, such as, "What could be the synthesis of these two kinds of pain? What could help us to understand one another better?" No answers came. That night I asked the powers of the dream world to show me or give me information concerning the wounded relationship between men and women and how we might come to terms with one another. The following dream was given the next morning.

> A woman who teaches clay sculpture stood in a courtyard. She held several clay scepters in her arms which she had made. She leaned down and stuck each one in the earth, forming a circle. Each scepter was topped with a face of the Fool, and painted gold.

My dream told me that one way to work with the "communication gap" between men and women is to get our Fools, our inner clowns, in touch with one another. We know from our own experience that this works with other areas of our lives. Perhaps it will help also with the very troubled relationships between the sexes in our present society.

A Playful Story of Fear or A Fearful Story of Play

Blue and Argus were in the shopping mall, trying to finish their last minute shopping, along with ten million other people. It was taking them a long time to do their shopping, because they would stop and give out balloons and hugs to so many people. Lucky for Blue and Argus that they were operating on "clown time," so they were in no rush. At least that is what Blue thought.

Argus decided he was in a hurry to go upstairs to a department store. He jumped on an escalator, and motioned for Blue to join him. Blue raced up to the first step and froze. From somewhere in the back of her mind, behind the makeup and pink hair, Blue remembered that Pat doesn't like escalators. She always hesitates before getting on one, counting the steps as they appear, and waiting for the third or fourth one before she gets on. Blue stood there counting steps, enjoying the security of the solid floor beneath her pink Nikes, trying to get up her courage to step onto the escalator, and wondering where this fear comes from.

Suddenly she heard Argus' kazoo. He was already at the top and motioned for her to look behind. Blue was amazed to see so many people in line behind her. They were waiting to get on the escalator, and they were not smiling. They didn't even look friendly. So with brave effort, Blue stepped onto the first step, deciding to save the deep contemplation for later. She was proud of herself, and Argus was at the top clapping his hands for her.

However, the people in line behind her were not cheering for her brave effort. It hurt Blue's feelings to know that they were unhappy with her. When she jumped off the escalator, Argus was waiting for her with a proud grin, and she felt safe again, but she also felt like crying.

With loud "Boo-hoos," Blue sat on the floor in a corner, as Argus tried to comfort her with a large red handkerchief. She felt a tap on her shoulder. A small boy was standing next to her. "Clown," he said, "I don't like moving stairs, too." Blue gave him a big hug. She was smiling again. It was good to know someone understood her fear.

The Archetype of the Fool
An extra added attraction!!

Argus, help! where are you when I need you the most?

(TAP ON SHOULDER) **There you are, you funny clown. You look fabulous in your top hat with flowers, tuxedo shirt with rainbow ribbons in the front, black**

pants and those gorgeous gold tennis shoes. I've missed you. We have an assignment. We have an article to write about this 'clowning around' we do together. How about some of your ingenious and imaginative ideas?

(ARGUS PUTS FINGER TO HIS HEAD — THINKS — LOOKS AROUND AND BEGINS TO SNORE.)

ARGUS, COME ON, DON'T DO THAT!

(ARGUS YAWNS.) **Please talk to me!** (ARGUS MAKES A SLICING MOTION ACROSS HIS THROAT AS IF HIS VOCAL CORDS HAVE BEEN CUT.) **All right, I know you can't speak. So do something that shows what clowning means to us — really means.**

(ARGUS PULLS OUT A PAPER HEART AND SMILES IN A FLIRTING MANNER.)

AR-GUS! Get serious! We have to be more intellectual, like explain the psychological and symbolic meaning behind the Archetype of the Fool and its importance throughout the history of mankind as a truth bearer. We need to say how the clown is in all of us and how the clown brings about transformation and a closer relationship to the God-space within us.

Argus, where are you? Come out right now from that closet and stop playing "When the Saints Go Marching In" on that noisy kazoo.

(ARGUS BOWS HIS HEAD AND BEGINS TO SNIFFLE AND BLOT HIS EYES WITH A HUGE HANDKERCHIEF.)

Argus, please, I didn't mean to hurt you. Let's talk about fun. What's the most fun you ever had? (ARGUS PRETENDS TO RIDE A SCOOTER.) **Oh, yes, I remember you rode a scooter up and down hospital halls.** (HE STOPS 'SCOOTERING' AND BEGINS TO BLOW BUBBLES.) **That's enough. Let's get back to business. We need to talk about the essence of clowning as being child-like and close to God.** (ARGUS STARTS TO HUM

When right is left, and left is wrong ???

(THE DOORBELL RINGS. ARGUS DASHES TO THE DOOR. HE USHERS IN ANOTHER CLOWN AND MAKES AN INTRODUCTION WITH A LOW SWEEPING BOW. THIS CLOWN IS DRESSED IN PINK, PINK COTTON CANDY HAIR, PINK OVERALLS, PINK POLKA-DOTTED SHOES AND PINK LACE GLOVES.)

Well, what's your name? (SHE POINTS TO A BLUE CIRCLE PINNED TO HER SHIRT.) **Blue circle?** (TWO HEADS SOLEMNLY SHAKE "NO".)

Blue dot? ("NO" AGAIN.) **Just plain Blue, the color?** (TWO HEADS, COMPLETE WITH GRINS, NOD "YES") **Well, great. I'm trying to say what clowning means, and I'm sent this? I give up!**

(BLUE PULLS OUT A MIRROR THAT HAS NO GLASS AND BEGINS TO POWDER HER NOSE.) **Oh, moan! This is the last straw!** (ARGUS HANDS ME A TOY CAMEL.)

Oh, me — Oh, me — this isn't funny. Being a clown is serious. It's a pathway to spiritual enlightenment and higher consciousness! (ARGUS AND BLUE BOTH FALL TO THE FLOOR, PRETENDING TO PRAY, AND THEN COLLAPSE AS IF THEY HAVE FAINTED.)

SILENCE. . .

MORE SILENCE. . .I BEGIN TO THINK ABOUT DEATH. . .

I've got it! I'll write about when you put on white face, you die to your ego and the colors represent being born to your Higher Self. That's it! Hallelujah!

Argus? Blue?

(THEY'VE GONE. I RUN TO THE WINDOW AND THERE THEY ARE OUTSIDE SWINGING ON A SWING SET! I THROW UP THE WINDOW AND SHOUT FOR THEM TO COME IN. THEY STOMP INTO THE ROOM.) **Look, I'm doing all the thinking and you're doing all the playing—totally unfair!** (THEY SLOUCH TO CHAIRS AND I SUGGEST THAT WE USE

REFERENCE BOOKS TO FIND SOME INFORMATION. THEY RUN TO THE BOOK SHELVES AND RETURN WITH ARM LOADS OF BOOKS. ARGUS TAKES NOTES WITH A THREE-FOOT PEN, AND BLUE PUTS ON GLASSES WITH NO LENSES, STARTS TO READ, TEARS OUT PAGES, TOSSES THEM OVER HER SHOULDER, CHEWS BUBBLE GUM WHICH SHE PUTS BEHIND HER EAR AS IT LOSES ITS FLAVOR, AND READS FRANTICALLY. THEY LOOK AT ONE ANOTHER AND SHAKE THEIR HEADS.)

Nothing? You can't define a clown?

(BLUE HOPS UP, BEGINS TO DANCE AND HANDS ME THE DICTIONARY UPSIDE DOWN. I TURN IT ARIGHT AND SHE POINTS TO A WORD. THE WORD IS **LOVE**. HER FACE IS GLOWING.)

Love? <u>That's</u> being a clown? It's a well-worn overworked word that doesn't mean anything anymore! (ARGUS HANDS ME A DUNCE CAP.) **Look, how do <u>you</u> talk about love?**

(ARGUS MAKES FLYING, TWIRLING MOTIONS AROUND THE ROOM. BLUE HUGS HERSELF. THEY HUM, "HAPPY BIRTHDAY, HAPPY BIRTHDAY TO YOU." ARGUS CHANGES MY CAP TO A PAPER CROWN AND DUSTS ME FROM HEAD TO FOOT WITH A FEATHER DUSTER. THEN FROM THEIR TOY BAG THEY PULL OUT A STRING OF CHRISTMAS LIGHTS AND WRAP THEM AROUND ME. ARGUS PLUGS THEM IN AND I'M LIT LIKE A CHRISTMAS TREE, WHILE BLUE PINS BRIGHTLY COLORED BALLS ALL OVER ME. OH'S AND AH'S ARE HEARD IN THE BACKGROUND. BLUE PLACES TINSEL IN MY HAIR. THEY CLAP AND DANCE AROUND ME.)

SUDDENLY, I KNOW —
THERE IT IS —
THAT *FEELING* —
THAT UNDEFINABLE

UNEXPLAINABLE
MYSTERIOUS FEELING
IN KNOWING THAT WORD
LOVE
AND ALL THAT IT IS.

Thank you, Argus. Thank you, Blue.
I am far richer because of you!

VIII.

Love and Fear

Love and fear are entwined, two vines twisted, one around the other. Recognizing and experiencing love makes us vulnerable to fear. If we are honest and open about one feeling, we will be open, and forced to be honest, about the other.

There are moments in which we experience complete and perfect love, while at other times fear overtakes us with panic and despair. By dealing with our fears we can find love returning us to the circle and the Center Ring of our lives. The clown helps us to see our fears for what they are and gives us the ability to approach them with a lighter and more humorous touch.

Fear diminishes, while love empowers. Through the clown, a new symbol with universal appeal, the child in us is waiting to take up the adventure and look at life with eagerness.

So, of what are we afraid? Failure, pain, isolation, death—our lists can be lengthy as well as heavy. Elizabeth Kubler-Ross tells us that we are born with only two natural fears, of loud noises and of falling. If this is so, then from where have all our fears come?

They have been taught to us by parents, friends, experiences. We have been faithful students of FEAR 101. Love is the Universal Force, but we are taught to hate. Using fear as a tool, we are taught to hate different cultures, people of different colors, different religions, differences in general—learned fears instead of learned loves.

The clown's white face, the death mask symbolizing loss of ego, takes away color, sex, race, superiority. Our clowns can help us see our foolishness over all these issues that our culture emphasizes.

With humor and with a love for ourselves and others, we learn ways to cope with our fears. In our chapter on the clown workshop, in the Imagery section, we saw how Marilyn—with the help of her friends—grappled with her fears and was thereby helped greatly. We can adjust to any fear as long as we can give it a name. Honestly naming a fear helps us learn to live with it amiably.

Clowns challenge us to look at our fears. We know a priest who allows liturgical clowns at some of the services. These clowns participate in the service, sometimes miming a gospel lesson or encouraging church members to become more involved in the service. He confided that although he supports this ministry, clowns make him uncomfortable. Asked why, he replied, "They make me feel I have to do something but I'm not sure what."

For someone who is used to being in control, accepting clowns is a difficult task. Clowns remind him of his fear of not being in control. Through being open to the clown ministry in his church, he works in a loving way with his fear.

You are familiar with the two masks which symbolize theatrical arts—the mask of comedy, the mask of tragedy. We usually think of clowns as comic figures, but they also have a tragic side. They can respond to our joys, to our sorrows, in deep and subtle ways. In these pages you have seen the clown as teacher and healer, ready to spread smiles and to dry tears. The clown reminds us that there are not always answers, but there is always a silent, loving presence.

Jean used her clown as a vehicle for reframing an unhappy childhood and transforming her fears. For Jean, a timid, unassuming woman, even attending a clown workshop, which she was doing at the suggestion of her therapist, was an act of courage. She was shy and hesitated to participate in the game playing or sharing of the Beginning Clowning workshop. Yet she hung in there. During guided imagery, she felt upset because she couldn't envision images or colors. We talked after the first workshop, giving her encouragement, as she said she'd had a good time, and admitted she had a fantasy of attending birthday parties as a clown. She signed up for the Intermediate Clowning workshop.

It was during that workshop that she experienced great insight. One of our exercises that day was to draw a picture of your childhood house. As she looked at her finished picture of a house with no windows or doors, Jean saw that she was trapped in her childhood house. She was able to share with the group that her mother was a schizophrenic. Her childhood had been devastating. There was no laughter, only fear of her mother and of her mother's violent attacks, and the desire to protect her younger siblings from the mother's wrath.

Fellow participants gave her encouragement to look at her fears and anger. They gave her permission to vent her anger at the injustices poured out on a little girl, and to express her fears that as an adult and as a mother she would some day be like her mother.

Once the rage and fear were given names, she could confront them. True, the past can never change, but we do have the ability to give ourselves new pictures. We asked Jean to draw a picture of an ideal childhood house. She looked at the finished product with amazement. It looked like the house she now lives in. There are lots of windows and flowers all around. As she looked at the reframed picture many of her fears of putting her own children through the same experience were resolved. She recognized that, in spite of the nightmares she had experienced as a child, she was giving her own children the love and attention she—like every child—had craved.

In a later guided imagery, Jean saw herself as a clown, laughing and entertaining children with puppets and balloons. Since then, Jean has learned to laugh out loud. She has developed a super clown character and whenever we clown with her, the children flock around her for attention.

Jean was able to use the clown to unlock her worst fears. She continues to use the clown to express her love for children and for herself.

Jean had a wealth of courage. For her, the clown was the spring board to reach what was always hers, always ours. What gives any of us that courage? It is simply LOVE. It is the feeling of being connected to other people. That is the net under the wire, giving support to the great balancing, the enormous risk-taking we all experience.

We have come to believe that there is a special energy of love that can exude from our very pores, our living cells, and can penetrate into realms we do not yet comprehend. The more we give up our egos, the more we see the essence of that special force. We have found that, as mystics and sages have taught, Love can heal. Love is that for which we yearn the most, that which we long to give. Our cultured, surface selves can be blocked off from the experience, the possibilities of love. But the clown is ever present, ever open to when it will mysteriously and magically appear.

The clown is a universal symbol, not tied to any culture, accessible to all humanity. We see the clown as "go-between" in international affairs, a global unifying symbol, THE PEACEMAKER. In an imagined future where the abilities of the clown are put to use, we can foresee clowns at the White House, entertaining dignitaries, giving them hugs, handing them paper hearts. Imagine Blue and Argus at the airport, greeting foreign ambassadors and rolling out tiny red carpets as they descend from the plane.

Maybe each country could have a "Laugh Representative" to challenge us into seeing which country can laugh the loudest and smile the longest. Maybe the Statue of Liberty will be replaced by a clown with its arms thrown out to embrace all mankind, and its head lit and smiling as it stands in the harbor. Perhaps each country will send its own clown envoy into outer space.

As you can see, our fantasies are building higher AND **HIGHER.** But we have a serious hope that this universal symbol, this clown, can be taken seriously and used, not only for our own personal centering, but for world-wide centering, world-wide peace.

The clown was once the court-jester who bore the Truth to the king. The clown was sacred among primitive tribes. We feel that, though in today's society the role of the clown does not receive this same recognition, it still holds great promise and hope for us as a culture and as a world. Can we move forward, broken umbrellas and rubber chickens in hand, faces and costumes bright with color, and filled with love abounding? Is this just a fantasy? We hope not.

Blue and Argus have come full circle. This is a time of celebration, for we have come to the end of our book, which is also the beginning. In creation there is no end and no beginning, for everything is connected in the force that keeps us balanced on the high wire in THE CENTER RING.

The Ending and the Beginning